PENELOPE
THE GLASS
CASTLE
SHARON E. McKAY

PENELOPE
THE GLASS
CASTLE
SHARON E. MCKAY

PENGUIN
CANADA

PENGUIN CANADA

Published by the Penguin Group

Penguin Books, a division of Pearson Canada, 10 Alcorn Avenue, Toronto, Ontario, Canada M4V 3B2

Penguin Books Ltd, 80 Strand, London WC2R 0RL, England

Penguin Putnam Inc., 375 Hudson Street, New York, New York 10014, U.S.A.

Penguin Books Australia Ltd, 250 Camberwell Road, Camberwell, Victoria 3124, Australia

Penguin Books India (P) Ltd, 11, Community Centre, Panchsheel Park, New Delhi – 110 017, India

Penguin Books (NZ) Ltd, cnr Rosedale and Airborne Roads, Albany, Auckland 1310, New Zealand

Penguin Books (South Africa) (Pty) Ltd, 24 Sturdee Avenue, Rosebank 2196, South Africa

Penguin Books Ltd, Registered Offices: 80 Strand, London WC2R 0RL, England

FIRST PUBLISHED 2002

1 3 5 7 9 10 8 6 4 2

NATIONAL LIBRARY OF CANADA CATALOGUING IN PUBLICATION

McKay, Sharon E.

Penelope : the glass castle / Sharon E. McKay.

(Our Canadian girl)

For ages 8–12.

ISBN 0-14-331207-3

I. Title. II. Title: Glass castle. III. Series.

PS8575.K2898P462 2002   jC813'.6   C2002-901326-7
PZ7

Visit Penguin Canada's website at **www.penguin.ca**

To Victoria (Tori)

Middle sister,

second

to none.

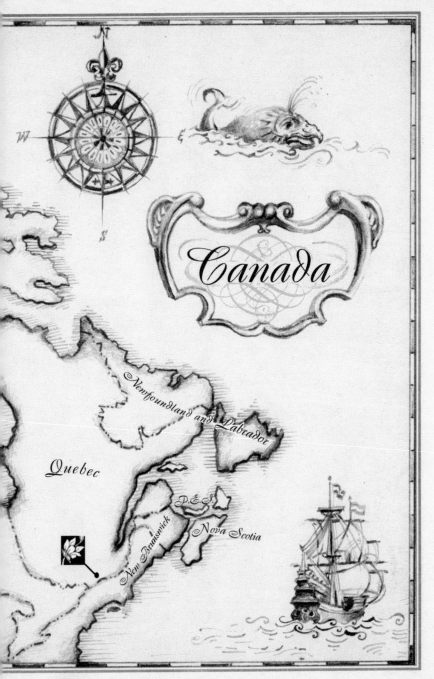

Canada

Quebec

Newfoundland and Labrador

P.E.I.

New Brunswick

Nova Scotia

 Marks the location of the story

FOREWORD
SPRING 1918

ACROSS THE SEA, THE GREAT WAR CONTINUES AS IT has for almost four years. The Germans are making advances, and it's whispered that the tide might be turning. Could the unthinkable happen? Could Germany win the war?

Meanwhile, Halifax is still reeling from the greatest man-made explosion ever to occur on earth to date. Two ships, one containing explosives bound for the war, collided in the Halifax Harbour destroying everything for kilometres. The explosion ripped through the North End of Halifax, flying glass blinded and killed, fires erupted, and finally, the very next day, a snowstorm blanketed the city.

More than three months have passed since that grim day. Housing is hard to find and the spread of disease is a concern. Papa is constantly worried about Penny, Emily, and baby Maggie. Penny's grandmother, Mrs. Penelope Underhill, has asked Papa to send the three girls to live with her in Montreal. Although Grandmother has never approved of Papa, Penny, Emily, and Maggie are still her granddaughters. Papa wants all his girls to be safe and healthy and he wants Penny to have a chance to go to the best schools, maybe university someday. But the last thing Penny wants is to leave Halifax and Papa.

CHAPTER N° 1

"Papa, you promised. You said that we'd stay together. You promised." Penny's fists were clenched so tightly that her nails bit into her palms. How could he? How could he send her away?

"Penny, lower your voice." Papa's eyes never left the mug of tea that sat on the rough wooden table in front of him.

"I won't be quiet. I won't." But even as Penny spoke, she could sense Mrs. O'Hara's nosy children eavesdropping behind the curtain. It wasn't even a proper curtain; it was just an old blanket that hung over a cord dividing the kitchen in two. Mrs. O'Hara and her three children lived downstairs, while Papa, Penny, Maggie, and Emily lived in two big rooms upstairs. She knew it was kind of Mrs. O'Hara to give up the bedrooms, but sharing the broken-down house with another family was awful.

They had no place else to live. There was precious little housing available in the North End of Halifax after the explosion in the harbour. Their own house had been destroyed, and now they had to make do. Besides, it was just temporary, until Papa built their new home in the summer.

"Penny, put on your coat. We'll go for a walk." Papa's voice was low and steady.

"What will happen to Maggie and Emily? Who will take care of them?" She mustn't cry. She mustn't!

"That's enough! Meet me outside."

Papa stood up, yanked his coat from the hook and made his way out into the crisp March morning.

It was all Penny could do not to shout after him. Oh, she hated this war. Hated it. If there were no war, then the *Imo* and the *Mont Blanc* wouldn't have crashed into each other, and Billy Hanson would still be alive. She could see him still, running towards the port to see the fire. Then came the explosion, and he was never found! And if it weren't for the explosion they would still be in their own house. And Papa wouldn't be breaking his promise and sending her away.

"Penny?" Five-year-old Emily poked her blond head around the curtain. "Where are you going?" She plugged her mouth with her thumb.

"Stay with Maggie, Emily." Penny gave her sister a weak smile.

"Maggie is sleeping."

"That's good. You stay with her. I'll be right back."

Two of Mrs. O'Hara's children, one as dirty as the other, came around the curtain and grinned. Penny sighed. It was hard finding enough hot water to keep themselves clean, but this lot hardly made the effort. Still, it didn't do to criticize. After all, Mrs. O'Hara had lost her husband in the explosion.

Papa stood out on the road, one hand cupping a pipe, the other dug deep into a pocket. Penny buttoned up her old coat and felt the soft fur collar hug her neck. It was the last thing her mother had made for her. Not long after, Mama had given birth to Maggie, and then died. That was a year and a half ago. The coat was too short by half—the sleeves came up past her wrists— and there were some stains that wouldn't come out, but she wouldn't give it up. She wouldn't.

"Let's walk." Papa set out, past burnt homes, down a rutty road made dirtier by the lumps of sooty snow piled up on either side.

Penny dragged her feet. There was nothing he could say to her, nothing she wanted to hear.

"Careful!" Papa reached out and pulled her in close as a horse-drawn sleigh glided past. Penny could feel his strong arms protecting her. She wanted to throw her own arms around him and plead, Don't, Papa. Don't send me away. I love you. But all Penny could manage was stony silence.

"Hear me out, darlin'. This is no fit place for any of you. What would happen, do you think, if Maggie or Emily got sick?"

A shudder went down Penny's spine.

"I have to work very hard. This city needs every builder it's got. But first I have to keep my wee girls safe." Papa turned and faced her squarely. "My sister in Toronto will take Maggie and Emily. You will go to Montreal and live with your grandmother. It's final. I've already posted the letters telling them of your arrival." Papa paused, as if steeling himself for what was to come. "And, I've bought the train tickets."

Penny sucked in her breath. He'd already bought the tickets! Didn't her opinion matter at all?

"Why can't I go to Toronto, too? Why?"

"My sister wanted all three of you, and so did your grandmother. It's a hard thing, splitting you up, but taking on three girls is too much of a burden for either of them. Try and understand."

Tears bottled up in her throat. She swallowed hard. This couldn't be happening. Not after all they had been through.

"Darlin'," Papa said, his voice soft with his Irish accent, "your Aunt Colleen is in Montreal. Sure, haven't ya always loved her, and she you. Come fall you'll go to a good school, and . . ."

"Fall!" Penny nearly stumbled. "Not that long!"

Penny spun around and ran down the street, ran as fast as she could. Ran and ran until her sides were splitting and her lungs gasped for air. How could he be doing this? How? She threw herself into a sooty snowbank and covered her eyes with her hands. He was sending them away for good!

CHAPTER N° 2

"We'll be fine, just fine." Miss Fisher seemed to be the cheery sort. Young, with rosy cheeks, she wore a hat tilted at a jaunty angle and sat like a prim red apple in the first-class compartment of the train. "Come, Maggie dear." She smiled in a sticky-sweet way. "Sit on my lap." Miss Fisher scooped Maggie out of Papa's arms and bounced the bewildered Maggie on her knee. They had the coach all to themselves.

"Awfully kind of you to care for them on the journey," said Papa. He had a flushed, tired look about him. But then, none of them had slept much last night.

"My pleasure." Miss Fisher beamed and Penny scowled. Miss Fisher had been gushing over Papa for the past hour. It wasn't right. So what if ladies like Miss Fisher had no one to marry on account of so many young men getting killed in the war. Penny bunched up her mouth until it was a hard, puckered bud. Papa would never marry again. He had said so. Then it occurred to her, he had also said he wouldn't send her away.

Papa picked up Emily and gave her a long hug, like he was trying to get the feel of her, like he'd never see her again. Penny thumped down on the seat opposite. The last three days had passed in an angry blur. Just shopping, shopping, shopping. She wouldn't let Papa buy her anything. Not so much as a hatpin. Emily and Maggie were all decked out in new dresses and coats with fur trim, hats, muffs, and lace-up boots. They were too little to know what was really happening.

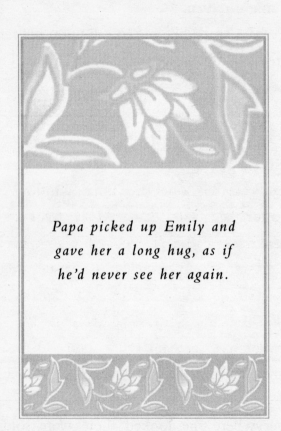

Papa picked up Emily and gave her a long hug, as if he'd never see her again.

They were being packed off! Sent away! They were leaving Halifax with no mention of when they might return.

"Perhaps you'd like me to call upon my return and tell you all about our little trip?" Miss Fisher spoke to Papa in a singsong voice.

"Yes," Papa said absent-mindedly while heaving, then arranging, their bags on the overhead luggage rack.

Penny stared out the train window. The explosion had badly damaged the train station, but the tracks had been repaired quickly, because all the soldiers from across Canada—supplies, too—arrived by train before boarding the ships for Europe. Mr. Shirley, her teacher, said that the war had made Halifax the third-most important port in the Empire. He said that like it was something to be proud of.

Everywhere she looked there were soldiers. Blank-faced young men in high-backed, wicker wheelchairs, nurses behind. Others leaning on crutches or canes. Plenty worse off than that.

Empty sleeves or pant legs, empty eyes and faces.

"I hate this war," Penny muttered under her breath.

"What did you say?" Papa bent down in front of her.

"Nothing."

"Penny, darlin', Mrs. O'Hara packed you a snack. You'll eat it, won't you?"

Eat? How could she eat? What was he talking about? She was losing her family and her home!

"I love you with all my heart." He took her hands in his.

She wouldn't cry. She wouldn't.

"Can ya' understand what it is to love someone so much that you're willing to part with them?" Papa's voice crackled. He was bone-weary.

Penny curled up on the seat and made herself small. Papa didn't love her, and he didn't love Emily or Maggie, either. If he loved them, he wouldn't be sending them away.

The locomotive's whistle gave a blast, followed by the slamming of doors, one after another—

bang, bang, bang—like slaps to the face.

"Penny?" Papa sounded as though he was in pain.

Penny wouldn't look at him. She wouldn't.

Hat in hand, Papa left the train as Miss Fisher scooped up Maggie, plopped her on her lap, and took up a post by the window. She picked up Maggie's tiny hand and waved it frantically in Papa's direction.

"Say bye-bye. Say bye-bye," prattled Miss Fisher.

Maggie's bewilderment turned to alarm. She leaned forward and pressed her face hard against the glass, and for a minute Penny thought she might speak. Emily, too, leaned against the window. Her nose left a fairy-breath imprint on the glass. She curled her hand into a sad, slow wave.

Papa, tears welling up in his eyes, stood on the platform and waved goodbye to his daughters.

Papa, Papa, please don't do this. Please don't send us away! Penny wanted to scream, to beat her hands against the window. Still, she couldn't bring herself to so much as look in Papa's direction.

The engine gasped, seemed to shudder, then slowly lurched out of the station. As the train gathered steam and finally made an arc at the foot of Richmond Bluff, Halifax was lost to her.

"There now." Miss Fisher plopped Maggie down on the seat beside Penny and dusted her hands. Her cheery smile turned into a frown. "We've a long trip ahead of us and I don't want any nonsense. Emily, whatever is wrong with you?"

Emily made little whimpering sounds as she curled up on the other side of Penny.

"She's just afraid. She's only five," Penny snapped as she put protective arms around her sisters. Little red apple indeed, Miss Fisher was a prune!

"Well, there's nothing to be afraid of and no sense crying over spilt milk. At least this one doesn't say anything." Miss Fisher looked over at the mute, wide-eyed Maggie.

"It's not her fault." Penny glared at Miss Fisher. "She hasn't spoken since the explosion."

"What age would she be?" Miss Fisher peered at the baby.

"She's one and a half."

"Well, you know what they say, children should be seen but not heard. Now, let's see . . ." Miss Fisher took a note from her bag, perched thin, wiry glasses on her nose, and read out loud, "Train departs at 7:15." She consulted a watch that hung from her smart, navy-blue travelling outfit. "Right on time. Good. We should arrive at Digby at precisely 1:40 and transfer to the Canadian Pacific steamship for the three-hour crossing to Saint John, New Brunswick. Are you listening, Penelope?" Miss Fisher peered over her glasses and glared hard at her. But, Penny thought, why should she listen? What did she care?

"Emily, do stop that whimpering. Now, where was I? We arrive in Montreal at Windsor Station at 8:30 in the morning. Excellent. Your grandmother, I suppose, will meet you. Then your sisters and I will carry on to Toronto." Miss Fisher leaned across the gulf between the seats. "I hear that your grandmother is one of the wealthiest women in Montreal." The very thought seemed to give her some pleasure, although Penny couldn't think why.

Satisfied that everything was in order and on schedule, Miss Fisher tucked the paper back into her handbag, drew two frighteningly long knitting needles from a cloth bag at her feet, and proceeded to click-clack them together to the rhythm of the train.

Penny hugged her sisters. In twenty-five hours, their lives would change forever.

CHAPTER N°. 3

"Montreal. Next stop, Montreal." The porter's voice vibrated down the train.

Penny sat bolt upright. Emily sat beside her, and Maggie, too, both propped up like china dolls in a shop window. They were all blurry-eyed. They had slept in bunks during the night, but still, the three girls hadn't slept well. But then with Miss Fisher's snoring, it was surprising that anyone on the entire train could sleep.

"It's time. Get yourself sorted out, Penny." Miss Fisher was all business.

"Penny, don't go!" Suddenly panicked, Emily lunged towards her big sister.

"Oh, Emily, don't cry." Penny held her tight and tried to stifle her own tears, which rose in the back of her throat with lightning speed.

"Enough nonsense." Miss Fisher slid the compartment door open and bellowed down the hallway, "Porter! Porter!"

"Yes, ma'am?" A porter appeared at the door.

"Please see to Miss Penelope Reid's bag. Off you go, Penelope. Stand by the exit. No need to cause upset."

Don't cry. Don't cry, Penny told herself as she hugged Maggie and Emily, and then Emily and Maggie.

"It will be fine. You'll see," she whispered into her sisters' ears. "Papa's sister will take good care of you. I know she will. And I'll write. I'll write every day."

"Nooooo." Emily wrapped her arms around Penny's neck.

"Emily, let go. It's going to be fine." But Emily would have none of it.

"Come to me!" Miss Fisher tugged at Emily's waist.

"Nooooo!" Emily hung on to Penny's neck even harder.

Penny gasped and gagged.

Miss Fisher gave one mighty yank, Emily let go, and the two went hurtling onto the far seat.

"Penny. I want Penny!" Emily, screaming, thrashed her arms about and kicked her feet. One hand sent the gasping Miss Fisher's hat into flight.

"Oh!" Miss Fisher howled. "You horrible child." Miss Fisher plunked Emily down hard on the seat.

"Ohhhhh," Emily sobbed.

"Emily, are you all right?" Penny fell on top of Emily and held her tight.

"Is she all right? What about me!" Miss Fisher scowled while retrieving her hat. "Leave immediately!" she shouted.

"I will not!" Penny stood straight and tall. "I'll stay with my sisters until the train stops!"

All the while, baby Maggie, her eyes wide,

watched the goings-on in silence.

Penny gathered up Maggie and pulled the sobbing Emily in close. "Now, listen to me carefully," she whispered. "I want you both to be very brave. Try not to cry."

How could she tell them not to cry when she felt like she was drowning in tears?

"Emily, you're the big sister now. You must take care of Maggie. You must."

Emily rubbed her eyes with two balled-up fists and bobbed her blond head.

"Papa says that Mama is always watching us and she'll look out for us. You remember?"

Emily nodded again, but she found it hard to remember Mama.

"I love you." She kissed each one, once, twice, three times.

The train glided to a grinding, squealing stop.

"Windsor Station." The porter slid open the compartment door.

Penny stood and turned to Miss Fisher. "There's no need for you to shout at my sisters ever again. And if you do"—Penny glared at Miss Fisher—"I shall tell my father that you . . . that you . . . snore!"

"How . . . how dare. . . ?" Miss Fisher sputtered.

"Goodbye." With her head held high, Penny walked out of the compartment, down the hall, and stepped off the train.

Don't look back, she repeated to herself. Don't look back.

CHAPTER N°4

The carpet bag knocked against her knees.
Penny grasped hold of the brass railing and
trudged up the steps from the tracks. It was
crowded. The mixed-up smells of coal, oil, and
grease made her stomach turn. Then, Windsor
Station! It nearly took her breath away. Why, it
had to be thousands of feet high! She didn't
know where to look. Up? Around? The ceiling
wasn't a ceiling at all but a massive dome, like
in a cathedral. And there was something else,
something she couldn't put her finger on. What

was it? And then she knew. There were hardly any soldiers! There were just regular people, rushing, talking. Maybe there was no war in Montreal.

"Penny, is that you?"

Penny spun around. "Aunt Colleen?" A young woman dressed from head to toe in a cream-coloured suit trimmed with white fur, and carrying a white fur muff, stood off to one side. On her head was a magnificent white fur hat.

"Penny, sweetheart!" Aunt Colleen swooped down on her and hugged her tight. She smelled like rosewater and Pears soap. "Come, let's get out of the way." She gently pulled Penny to one side as other passengers jostled past. "Now, let me look at you."

Penny looked down at her dirty boots, old cloth coat, and worn carpet bag. She felt ugly standing in front of her elegant aunt with the dark hair and brown, flashing eyes.

"How lovely you've become! What gorgeous red hair. I'm glad to see that the pretty colour is not fading."

"Papa says that the history of Ireland is in my hair," Penny whispered.

"In your hair and in those lovely green eyes. And look how tall you are. You're a beauty. Your mother would be so proud. But you're so pale. Have you eaten today?"

Penny, her eyes locked on her scruffy brown shoes, shook her head.

"What about last night?"

Again, she shook her head.

"Anytime yesterday?"

Penny said nothing.

"It's hard leaving home," her aunt murmured.

Penny just nodded.

"I understand. We'll get you home and Cook will make you up a late breakfast."

"Who is Cook?"

"Cook is . . . the cook!" Aunt Colleen sniffed, then dabbed the tip of her nose with a hanky. "I'm sorry. I have a bit of a cold. Come now. Arthur is outside with the car. He is your grand-mother's driver. He's getting on, but then he's been with the family for thirty years. You'll meet the rest of the staff after you have had a rest."

Staff? Grandmother? Fear came over her like a sharp wind. Up until now she'd really only been thinking about Papa and her sisters, and how mad she was.

"I must find a pillar box and mail this note to your father. He'll want to know that you have arrived safely."

True enough, once Aunt Colleen had posted her letter, they found old Arthur standing by a sleek, long automobile and holding the door open. Penny peered inside. The seat was black leather with a large fur rug spread across it. A window divided the driver from the passengers. It was dark in there.

"Come along. We don't have far to go." Aunt

Colleen took her hand and guided her in. "See?" She pointed up towards a hill in the distance. "It's called Mount Royal."

They drove through Montreal, past busy streets, and then up, up to what seemed like the top of the mountain. Everything in Montreal felt newer, cleaner, better. And, as the car strained to climb the hill, the houses became bigger, bigger even than the ones in the South End of Halifax.

"They call this area the Golden Square Mile," said Aunt Colleen. "Years ago, in the 1850s, wealthy businessmen wanted to get away from all the epidemics, overcrowding, and noises around the port, and so they began building houses on the side of the mountain. Here we are."

Penny looked up. The street signs read Pine Avenue and Peel Street. Then she looked across a lawn as big as a park. There stood a red-brick fortress. Great bay windows flanked a gigantic oak door, and the chimneys were as mighty as smokestacks. And towers! Real towers, like in the fairy-tale books!

"I can't go in there," whispered Penny.

"Whyever not?"

"It's a castle."

"It's your home, Penny."

"But, I'm not a princess."

CHAPTER N.º 5

"Ma'am." A maid, wearing a white cap and smart black dress covered by a starched white apron, opened the door and gave a small curtsy. She looked about sixteen, with a spray of freckles across her nose and nut-brown hair tucked under a cap.

"Where is Duncan, Sally?" Aunt Colleen spoke while removing her long, pale, kid gloves. They stood in a wood-panelled hall with a circular stairway on the right. There were doors everywhere, all closed.

"His mother's got the influenza, ma'am. He's gone home."

"I'm sorry to hear it. Sally, this is Miss Penny."

"Miss Penny." Sally curtsied and smirked at the same time.

What should she do? Penny curtsied right back. Sally muffled a giggle.

"Enough of that, Sally. Do tell Aunt Penelope that her granddaughter has arrived, and take Miss Penny's bag up to her room, please. Oh, and have Cook make up a plate of eggs and toast."

"Yes, ma'am." The maid gave another little curtsy, took their coats, and didn't so much leave as vanish.

"Penny, sweetheart, there's no need to curtsy to the servants. Just be polite and always considerate."

"Yes, Aunt Colleen." Her face grew hot. "Are there many more—I mean, more servants?"

"Yes. It's all a bit much, isn't it." Aunt Colleen smiled.

Penny nodded. One day ago she'd been just plain Penny Reid. Now she was Miss Penny, and she lived in a castle, and she was sure that she didn't feel at all like a princess was supposed to feel.

"Your grandmother was born in this house. Your grandfather was from Halifax, so when they married, grandmother moved there. Of course she came back a great deal. Your mama was born here, too, did you know that?"

Penny shook her head. Mama hadn't talked much about herself as a little girl. All Penny could remember her saying was that she was never really happy until she met Papa.

"After your grandfather died, your grandmother moved back here for good. He was my mother's brother, but my parents died years ago. I have only my brother, Robert, and thankfully he's out of the war now. Safe at last. I'm your grandmother's companion. There's not much other employment for an old spinster like me." Aunt Colleen gave a small laugh and again dabbed her nose with a hanky.

Penny looked up, startled. Aunt Colleen wasn't a spinster! Spinsters were old and creeky. Aunt

Colleen was young and the most beautiful woman Penny had ever seen. Except for Mama, of course.

"Your mother was not only my favourite cousin, she was my very best friend." Aunt Colleen gave Penny's hand a little squeeze, and together they walked across the hall to the drawing room.

"Mrs. Underhill is waiting, ma'am." Sally stood in front of what had to be the drawing-room door.

"I'm right here," Aunt Colleen whispered into Penny's ear.

The door swung open and there, sitting in a high-backed chair by a small fire, was the Queen. Well, she looked like the Queen. Penny drew in a breath.

"Come here, child. Let me look at you." The Queen, or rather Grandmother, motioned her forward. Penny shrank back, she couldn't help herself. "Are you deaf, child? I said, come here."

Slowly, Penny walked across a soft oriental rug.

She pressed her dress down with the palms of her hands and hoped her shoes were buried so deep into the rug that they wouldn't be noticed.

Grandmother took a pair of thin, wire-framed glasses out of a leather case, perched them on the end of her nose, and looked up.

"Good heavens!"

CHAPTER *N*o 6

"Good morning, Penelope. I trust you slept well?"

Grandmother sat at the head of a long, polished table. She didn't seem to require an answer, because she immediately went back to perusing a list by the side of her plate.

"Yes, thank you, Grandmother."

"You may sit here." Grandmother motioned to the chair nearest her. "In future, you'll remember that breakfast is served promptly at eight. Although, since I haven't set eyes on your aunt this morning, I can hardly berate you."

"Yes, Grandmother."

What did berate mean? Nothing good, of that Penny was sure.

"And how did you find your bedroom?" Grandmother spoke while writing.

"Aunt Colleen showed me where it was."

Sally, the maid, stood beside the buffet and pressed her lips together in an attempt to squelch a giggle. It didn't work.

"I mean, how is your bedroom?" Grandmother, who didn't seem to take any notice of Sally, glanced up over her glasses.

"It's very nice." No matter how hard she tried, Penny couldn't raise her voice above a whisper.

"Good."

Thing was, it wasn't nice. Not nice like a dress is nice, or an ice cream is nice. It was . . . she hadn't the words! The bed had great posts to it, and the mattress was so thick that it felt like sleeping on a cloud. And the furniture was old and heavy. And the room was as almost as big as Mrs.

O'Hara's whole house. And there were huge rugs on the floor and too many lamps to count and . . .

"Miss?"

Penny jumped. Sally was at her elbow with a platter of food. She had replaced her smirk with a face as blank as a plank. Penny looked at the tray. What should she do? Was she supposed to eat everything on the tray? Why, there were sausages and ham and enough scrambled eggs to feed ten people!

"Penny, why don't you help yourself to a sausage and some eggs?" Aunt Colleen glided across the breakfast room and sat opposite Penny. "I apologize for being late, Auntie," she said, as she spread a crisp linen napkin across her lap. Penny snatched up her own napkin and laid it over her lap. "It seems that Duncan's mother has taken a turn for the worse. Cook is making up a basket of food for the family. If it's all right with you, I'll have Arthur run it down to them this afternoon."

Grandmother cleared her throat but said nothing.

Sally cleared her throat too. Again, Penny looked at the platter. She took a deep breath, picked up the two large utensils and, carefully, aimed for a fat sausage. It escaped. Sally muffled a giggle. Grandmother hadn't noticed, thank goodness. She tried again. This time the sausage scurried across the platter like a tadpole in a pond. On her third try, Penny stabbed a sausage, then scooped a spoonful of scrambled eggs.

"Kippers?" Sally returned with a smaller platter of buttered kippers.

"No. I mean, no thank you."

"Now, Penelope"—Grandmother removed her thin reading glasses and placed them neatly by her plate—"I have engaged a music teacher and a general academic teacher. The dressmaker, Mrs. Hoffman, will arrive in an hour. I have given her a list. Do you need a spring coat?" Grandmother did not wait for a reply. "Sally, bring in Miss Penelope's coat."

"Yes, ma'am." Sally gave a quick curtsy and scurried from the room just as Aunt Colleen sneezed.

36

She took a deep breath,
picked up the two large
utensils and, carefully, aimed
for a fat sausage.

"Colleen, that cold of yours does not seem to be getting any better. Perhaps we should give the doctor a call."

"I'm fine, Auntie." Aunt Colleen took a sip of tea. Truth be told, Aunt Colleen didn't look the least bit well. Her face was flushed and her nose quite red.

"Oh!" Grandmother let out a gasp. "Oh!"

What was it? What was wrong?

Lying across Sally's arms was Penny's coat.

"Child, you were wearing that?" Grandmother was horrified.

"It's my coat. Mama made it . . ."

But she could say no more, as Grandmother's hand was now flying through the air.

"Burn it. Get rid of it."

"No," Penny cried. "No, I . . ."

"Don't be ridiculous, Penelope. You can't possibly be seen in that thing. It looks as though it has been through a war."

"It has," Penny whispered as Sally, and her coat, sailed out of the room. Tears stood behind her eyes. Penny blinked, and blinked again.

Aunt Colleen sneezed. "Excuse me, Auntie. I'll just run and get myself a clean hanky."

Aunt Colleen left the room and Penny and Grandmother were alone.

Grandmother perched her glasses back on her nose and continued to jot notes on her list.

Penny looked at her out of the corner of her eye. Grandmother was thin, her face pinched. Long lines streamed down from her forehead towards her nose, then circled her mouth. It was hard to tell how old she was, mostly because she wore a black, old-fashioned dress with a lace collar hugging her throat. And it was hard to tell what colour her eyes were—blue, maybe. Her hair was white, and with the morning sun coming through the window, it was sparkly.

"There." Seemingly satisfied, Grandmother laid down her pen. "Mrs. Hoffman will bring three or four ready-made dresses for alterations, along with fabric for the rest of your wardrobe. You'll be needing a dress immediately, as we will be attending Mrs. Meighen's house party tomorrow afternoon. I expect you to be on your best behaviour, Penelope. This will be your introduction to Montreal society, and I want you to make a good impression."

"Will Aunt Colleen be coming?" Penny's voice simply could not be raised over a whisper.

"Naturally. Assuming, of course, she gets rid of that cold. How very careless of her. She simply persists in doing war work at the hospital. Now, after your fittings, we will have lunch promptly at one. Your tutor, Mr. Davis, will arrive at two this afternoon. Your piano and musical theory will not begin until next week. I expect you to apply yourself diligently to your studies throughout the remainder of the spring and the entire summer. I haven't decided which school you will attend in the fall."

"No, no, I'll be home in the fall," Penny protested. She wanted to cry out, to yell, but all she could muster was a series of pitiful squeaks.

"This is your home, Penelope. And, in future,

while you are welcome to mention your sisters, please refrain from referring to your father. Oh, Colleen, you're back."

Aunt Colleen, her nose worse for wear, stood by the door.

"Mrs. Hoffman is here, Auntie. I had Sally show her into the upstairs sitting room."

"Very well. Colleen, if you would, tell her to add a coat to the list, and a hat, of course. I'll ring up Holt's and have some shoes and boots sent over. What size would you be, my dear?"

Penny twisted her scruffy shoes behind the legs of her chair. "I'm not sure."

"Speak up, girl!"

"I'm not sure, Grandmother." Penny tried to speak bravely, but the best she could manage was loudly.

"I'm not deaf. Colleen, have Mrs. Hoffman draw a pattern of her feet. Duncan can run down to the shop and pick out a few pairs."

"Remember, Auntie, Duncan is with his mother, and Sally has a great deal of work to do as it is. I'll be happy to pick up the shoes," said Aunt Colleen.

"Maybe it is best if you picked them out. You have excellent taste, my dear."

"Thank you, Auntie."

Grandmother stood, folded her napkin, and placed it beside her plate. "Penelope, I hope . . ." She dithered. "I'd like to think . . ." She paused. "I'm sure you'll be happy here." And with that, Grandmother turned abruptly and swept out of the room.

"Penny," Aunt Colleen said gently, "it's going to be fine. You'll see."

Again, Penny willed herself not to cry. What was happening to Emily and Maggie right now? Did they miss her as much as she missed them?

"Come on now, let's see to your new clothes." Aunt Colleen stood up and extended her hand.

"Papa gave me a store-bought dress just before the explosion. It was blue."

Colleen gave Penny's hand a squeeze as they made their way up the winding staircase.

CHAPTER N° 7

Penny wiggled her toes in her leather shoes with patent toecaps and yanked at the bow on her new, pale-yellow dress. All her new clothes were old-fashioned but then, Mrs. Hoffman was as ancient as Grandmother, and she said that young girls in society had to set a modest standard for others. What did that mean? Still, Penny liked the gold ribbon that held her hair back.

"Your coat, Miss Penny." Sally, her nose stuck on the ceiling, held up her new black velvet coat.

"Thank you." Penny kept her eyes low, not

daring to look at Sally directly.

"Hat and gloves." Sally held them out.

Penny pulled on a felt tam with velvet trim, and matching gloves. As the clock struck two, Grandmother came down the staircase. For the first time, Penny could see that Grandmother was, not beautiful like Aunt Colleen but—what was the word? Handsome, like royalty.

"Good." Grandmother looked Penny up and down. "You're much improved. Sally, has Arthur brought the automobile around?"

"Yes, ma'am." Sally curtsied as she held out Grandmother's fur coat.

"Then we'll be off." Grandmother put on her coat, then slipped her long, slender hands into kid-leather gloves.

"Where is Aunt Colleen?" Penny peered up the circular staircase. Her heart started to race.

"She is in bed. I knew that jaunt about town yesterday would make her cold worse. Sally, take her up a pot of tea and a hot water bottle. The doctor will stop by shortly."

Penny's heart sank into her shoes. How would she manage without Aunt Colleen!

"Sally, my muff!"

"Yes, ma'am." Sally held out a matching fur muff.

From the far corner of the sitting room came the muffled jingle of the telephone. It was kept in a small, wooden box on the floor because Grandmother thought the telephone an unsightly-looking instrument. Sally recoiled from the sound.

"Sally!" Grandmother was indignant. "Do something about that racket."

"Yes, madam." But Sally didn't so much as budge. She just stood, stiff as a board, with a look of terror in her eyes.

"Oh, for goodness' sake. It won't kill you." Grandmother piled her muff and gloves into Sally's arms and stomped back into the sitting room.

This was her chance. Penny bolted towards the stairs. With one hand on the banister, she swung around and began taking the steps, two, even three, at a time.

"Miss? Miss?" Sally ran to the bottom of the staircase and hissed. "Where are you off to?"

Panting, Penny stood on the upstairs landing. Which room?

"Aunt Colleen, where are you?"

She tried one door, then another, then another, all the while crying out, "Aunt Colleen?"

"Penny? Penny, is that you?"

Penny pivoted on her feet, then ran towards the sound of her aunt's voice. She burst into the room. Aunt Colleen, her eyes wide with alarm, bolted up in the large, four-poster bed.

"I can't go on my own. I simply can't! Please talk to Grandmother."

"Come here." Aunt Colleen held out her arms and Penny plunged headlong into them. "Now listen to me. You are the bravest little girl I know. Your father wrote me, you know. He told me all about the explosion. He's very proud of you."

Penny only buried her head deeper into Aunt

Colleen's arms. "Please tell Grandmother that I can't go, not alone!" She wasn't brave, not in the least.

"Come on now! You're going to have tea, for heaven's sake." Aunt Colleen gave Penny an encouraging smile. "You won't be eaten. They will serve food there!" Aunt Colleen laughed and petted Penny's hair. "Now, sit up. Straighten your hat. Smile, please."

Despite her best effort to be miserable, Penny grinned as she pushed her tam back on her head.

"I have something for you. I was going to save it for later, but . . . See that trunk over there?" Aunt Colleen pointed to a large blanket box in front of a bay window. "Go and open it."

Penny dried her face with the back of her hand, swung her legs over the side of the bed, and stumbled over to the box. Grasping two large handles, she heaved it open.

Her coat!

"You didn't think I'd let something as precious as that be tossed out, did you?" Aunt Colleen's smile was chased away by a cough.

"Thank you." The lid to the blanket box banged shut as Penny raced over to the bed and threw her arms around her aunt. "Oh, thank you."

"Now, stand up. Shoulders back." Aunt Colleen beamed. "Off you go now. Remember, you are the bravest girl I know."

Penny tried to smile but all she could manage was a tight grin.

"Miss! Miss!" Sally, distraught, stood at Aunt Colleen's bedroom door. "Hurry, miss. Don't keep your grandmother waiting."

Penny looked up at the maid. Had she been there all the time?

"Hurry, miss." Sally flapped her apron and shooed her forward as if she were a fly.

The two raced down the steps and stood by the front door. Grandmother was still shouting into the phone. It was hard to tell if she was angry or if the line was especially bad today.

"I want to say ..." Sally whispered without taking

her eyes off the sitting-room door, "it can't be easy coming to a place like this, on your own, like. And, well, I'll help you if I can."

Penny's mouth gaped open. If the earth had done a cartwheel Penny could not have been more astounded.

"That's settled." Grandmother came sailing out of the sitting room bent on making up for lost time. "Penelope, why is your mouth open? Close it, please."

Penny snapped her mouth shut so fast her teeth clicked.

"Sally, where is my muff?"

"Oh!" Sally, her face blazing red, gathered up the muff and gloves and handed them over. Suitably attired, and without another word, Grandmother breezed out the door and into the waiting car.

"Sally?" Penny turned back to the maid. "I . . ."

"Penelope, we are late. Come along."

"Go on now, you'll be fine," Sally whispered as Penny raced down the steps and into the waiting automobile.

"Blanket, ma'am?" Arthur stood on the curb holding several blankets.

"Arthur, you can be such an old lady. We're just going down the hill, for goodness' sake."

"Yes, ma'am." Arthur gave a little bow, got into the driver's seat, and set off down the road at a snail's pace.

"Now, Penelope, pay attention. It's important that you know just who is who in society. We don't want to ask embarrassing questions due to ignorance, especially in times of war. Do you see that house over there?"

Penny looked out the automobile window to a stone mansion that sat on the hill like a crouching, grey monster. How rich they must be!

"That is Ravenscrag. It belongs to Sir Hugh Montagu and his wife, Marguerite. I don't expect we'll met them at the Meighens', but should we, know that their son, Hugh Jr., was killed in battle recently. Their two young daughters, Anna and Gwendolyn, fifteen and seventeen respectively, went down with the *Lusitania*."

Penny held her breath. The *Lusitania* was the great British passenger ship sunk by the Germans in 1915. Over twelve hundred people were drowned off the coast of Ireland. Penny stared at the massive house. Three children—all dead! Was it possible to be rich and still have such terrible things happen?

"And that is Lord Atholstan's house." Grandmother sniffed. "Lord indeed. His name is Hugh Graham. Common journalist, I'd say. Thoroughly unlikeable. Founder of the *Montreal Star*—full of stuff and nonsense. Turn here, Arthur." Grandmother rapped the crook of her umbrella on the window that divided driver from passenger. "Over there is John Kenneth Ross's house. He's away at war, an officer with the Royal Canadian Navy. Good thing, too, what with inheriting all his father's millions. Maybe the war will give him some character. And over there, oh, it is hard to see from here—on McTavish Street, Alfred Baumgarten—German sympathizer, if you ask me. Don't bring up his name. Down here, Arthur." Again Grandmother rapped on the window. "There is the Herbert Molson house. He was hit in the head with a piece of shrapnel at the Battle of Mont Sorel. Very careless of him. Can't say it did him any lasting damage, he's still making ale. Most of the homes have had a son wounded or killed. Arthur, turn along McGregor Street."

"It's here, too," Penny whispered.

"Good heavens, girl, speak up."

"The war. I thought, maybe, it wasn't here."

"Whatever do you mean? All of Canada, all of the world, is at war. There's not a week that goes by that a friend's child isn't killed, or hopelessly wounded." Grandmother slumped back in her seat and, for a brief moment, looked tired. "We're a country of eight million. Almost 600 thousand of our boys are away at war now. How will we manage without our young men?"

CHAPTER N⁰ 8

"Ma'am?" Arthur looked up into the driver's mirror. The car stopped in the drive of a stone mansion on Drummond Street.

"Ah, here we are." Grandmother gathered herself together as Penny peered out the window.

"Ohh!" She nearly gasped. This house was the most beautiful of all. It wasn't as big as some of the others, but more—what was the word? Stately—that was it!

"Penelope, Mrs. Meighen's husband died in 1911. He was an Irishman, but a good one."

Grandmother alighted from the car.

An Irishman? "Grandmother, did you say Mr. Meighen was Irish?" Penny scrambled after her. So it was possible to be Irish and accepted by society people.

"Grandmother, about the Irish . . ."

"Penelope, straighten your hat." They walked up the stone steps. A massive wooden door mysteriously swung open when they reached the top.

"Thank you, Druthers." Grandmother spoke in a posh voice to the pointy-faced butler who took their coats and gloves. "This is my granddaughter, Penelope Reid."

"Very good, madam." Druthers bowed.

Penny looked around. It was hard to keep her head still. Papa built the insides of houses—the outsides, too, since the explosion in Halifax—but he'd likely never seen anything like this before. There was wood everywhere, dark and polished to a high sheen. The banister running up to the top floors—why, it was wider than two of her hands put together! And the windows—they were stained glass, like the ones in Grandmother's house, but much nicer.

"Penelope, keep your eyes in your head," Grandmother murmured under her breath.

"Yes, Grandmother."

"Penelope, how nice to see you." A large woman with pearls wrapped around her neck, wearing a dress of delicate pale lace, stood, regal and tall, in front of a small coal fire in a grand hall and smiled.

"Elsie, dear!" Grandmother and Mrs. Elsie Meighen gave each other a kiss on the cheek.

"This is my granddaughter, Penelope." Grandmother turned and extended her arm towards Penny.

"Penelope, is it? So, you were named after your grandmother." Mrs. Meighen spoke in a kind way.

"Yes, ma'am." It was odd, having the same name as Grandmother. Odd and unfair. "But I go by Penny Reid. Reid's an Irish name." Penny didn't have to look Grandmother's way to know that a scowl was on her face.

"Why, my name is Irish, too." Mrs. Meighen's beam matched Grandmother's scowl exactly. "I am delighted to meet you."

Should she shake hands or curtsy? What should she do? Penny's body had a mind of its own because, without her say-so, she curtsied.

"How lovely she is, Penelope," Mrs. Meighen said to Grandmother.

The two women turned and walked, arm in arm, into the grand salon. Penny scurried behind and tried really hard not to crane her neck in all directions. The grand salon was filled with polished furniture and fat sofas and chairs. Dozens of people, their hands holding delicate glasses, turned and nodded to Grandmother as they entered. A lady, dressed like a fairy, played a harp in the corner. There were servants, too, lots of them, all moving quietly among the guests like ghosts.

"Where is Colleen? We have a surprise for her," said Mrs. Meighen.

"Under the weather, I'm afraid," said Grandmother.

"That is a shame. Here is her surprise now."

Standing in the middle of the grand room was a soldier in full military dress. It was Robert, Colleen's brother!

CHAPTER N⁰ 9

"Aunt Penelope." *Robert placed his glass* on a tray and reached out for Grandmother.

"Robert, it is good to see you. Or should I say Major! But we thought that you were out of the army!"

Robert planted a smacking big kiss on Grandmother's cheek and, much to Penny's amazement, Grandmother turned pink! For a second she even thought she heard Grandmother giggle! No, no that was impossible. Her ears had to be playing tricks on her.

"Not entirely, Aunt Penelope. I was given the option to return to civilian life but I took an extended leave instead. And here's our Penny. What a beauty!" Uncle Robert took two big steps forward and swung Penny up in his arms. It was all she could do not to scream with delight. "Are you too big for a hug?"

"Robert, put her down. You're making a spectacle of yourself."

"Can't help myself, Auntie. I see a pretty girl and I just want to hug her." And he hugged her again. This time Penny did laugh out loud as her uncle put her gently back down.

"Hello, Uncle Robert." Penny turned pink.

"Uncle, is it? I thought we had dispensed with that ridiculous title. Uncles are all stuffy old men. Do you find me stuffy?" He shifted his eyes back and forth to all the old men around them.

"No." Penny laughed again.

"No indeed. And you are as pretty as a picture."

Now Penny's face had turned red, she was sure of it.

"Where is my beautiful sister?" He looked past them all to the door.

"She's caught herself a cold, but I daresay she'll see you anyway." Grandmother now sounded quite merry.

"I should hope so. I'm off to Halifax tonight, then on to France. I'm waiting for my orders now."

"France?" Grandmother was shocked. "But you've been wounded."

"I've signed on as an aide-de-camp, Aunt Penelope, assisting one of the senior officers. I'll be out of the fighting and safe enough."

"Oh, really, Robert, you're an officer. Surely you could have found yourself a better position, one in Ottawa perhaps. After all, you have done your duty." Grandmother frowned.

"My ol' foot, yes."

No one referred to Robert's foot. But then, except for a cane and a limp, no one would know that he had been injured. A shell took away half his foot—and three of his friends. It had landed in the communication trench. They had their hands wrapped around mugs of tea and were eating biscuits sent from home.

"Well, it's good to hear that you will not see action again. Come, Penelope, there is someone I'd like you to meet." Mrs. Meighen gently pulled Grandmother's elbow. "Robert, see that Penny gets a fruit punch."

"A punch and anything else she desires." Robert laughed again.

Penny looked up at his soft brown eyes and the light-brown hair that fell over his forehead, and she thought that he was the most handsome man she had ever met! Could he read her thoughts? She looked down at her shoes and vowed not to look at him again.

"A punch, please." Penny spoke to her shoes and half expected them to respond.

"A delicious red fruit punch for the most beautiful girl in the room. Come along. This house was built by the great Lord Mount Stephen himself. Do you know who he was?"

Penny shook her head.

"Lovely old fellow, they say. Born in Scotland. Lives in England now. He was one of the founders of the Canadian Pacific Railway, the railway that made us a country! This house is a work of art, but then"—Robert smiled down at her—"so was the railway. This is the conservatory. Stay put. I'll get you your punch." Robert flashed her another grin as he turned and left.

Penny found herself in a round, glassed-in room. Giant plants, with great flat leaves, reached up towards a glass dome. A fountain, spouting bubbles and spreading a cool mist, stood in the middle. And the floor was made of marble squares in intricate patterns.

"Here you go." Robert gave Penny a crystal cup filled with ruby-red punch.

"Sir." The butler appeared and held out a silver tray with an envelope on it.

"I was expecting this." Robert thanked the butler as he snatched up the letter and scanned it. "I'm to report immediately."

The war. It was always the war!

"Why are you going back to France if you don't have to?" She hadn't meant to blurt that out.

"Well, the only way I can think of to get out of this mess is to get on with it and win. Although, win or lose, the sooner it's over, the sooner we can all get back to living the lives we were born to live." Robert ruffled her hair and turned to leave.

Startled, Penny broke her vow and looked up.

"Are we losing the war?"

"At this particular moment, yes, we may well be. The Germans are on us." She had never, not once, heard anyone even suggest that losing the war was a possibility. "I must be off."

"Wait, what about Aunt Colleen? She'll want to see you." Penny lurched forward. The red liquid sloshed around in her crystal cup.

"Give her my love and tell her that I will be safe. Take good care of her for me. She loves you."

Penny felt a kiss land on her head, but by the time she looked up, Robert was gone.

"I say, Robert, where are you off to in such a hurry?"

Penny peered around the corner of the conservatory and back into the grand salon. A large, barrel-shaped man with a great handlebar moustache had Robert by the arm.

"I have my orders, sir," Robert said gruffly. "I must report immediately."

"Envy you, my boy. Itching to fight the Huns, are you?" The man threw his head back and laughed heartily.

"The only thing that itches in the trenches, sir, are lice. It's the number-one enemy. Lice, trench foot—the Germans come in a poor third, I'm afraid."

"I say, Robert, that's a bit much. Not very sporting." Another man, as thin and long as the first was short and round, blustered and sputtered. Foamy spittle collected around the corners of his mouth.

"What sport is there in men dying, sir?" Robert's voice was tense and sharp.

"You're sounding like one of those Frenchmen in Quebec City. Up in arms again last night, another one of their damnable demonstrations. Don't want to fight for les anglais, they say. Bunch of bloody cowards. Prime Minister Borden is right, we need conscription. If they won't join up of their own free will, arrest the lot, I say."

Who was talking now? Penny couldn't tell. Several more men, each with a glass in hand, had now formed a circle around Robert.

"Cowards, that's right! Take them out of their fields, take them out of their homes! Give them a gun, and if they don't shoot, we'll shoot them ourselves! Cowards, the lot of them!"

Penny brushed aside a large, leafy fern and stood on tiptoe. There was nothing to see except the backs of men, but there was something in the way Robert held his head that told her he was very, very angry.

"Quebec's 22nd Battalion preformed heroically, sir." Robert's voice bristled. "I was there in 1916 at the Battle of Courcelette. I can assure you, you'll not find a finer, more courageous regiment than the Van Doos. Most of the officers, and their men, were killed. Cowards? I think not, sir. But perhaps their mothers are tired of seeing their sons die for a cause so far removed from their own lives."

"I say there, Robert, you must not let your own injury cloud your thinking. God and country, and all that."

"We'll win this war," said the round man with the handlebar moustache.

"We've invested too much money to lose now. We just have to keep up our spirits," added another male voice.

"I think the cost should be measured in human lives, not dollars, sir." Robert's voice was rising.

"Enough of this talk, gentlemen."

This was a lady's voice. But whose? If only she could see better.

"My apologies, madam. I must take my leave." All Penny could see was Robert's head as he made a small, polite bow.

"Perhaps, gentlemen, you might want to enjoy your cigars in the upstairs library?" It was Mrs. Meighen.

How unfair. What did those fat old men know about war? About bombs going off and innocent people being blown to bits? Cities in Europe were being bombed, just like Halifax. Homes gone, children gone! And what did they know about all those wounded soldiers that came back off the boats with bits missing off them, with empty, sad eyes? Penny spun around. Perhaps she could wave to Robert from the window? She tilted forward and, oh, her foot caught. Oh, oh! The crystal cup filled with red punch flew up, up into the air! It seemed to hover there for a moment. Light shone through it, as though it were a prism. And then it crashed and splintered into a million gleaming pieces on the marble floor.

CHAPTER N° 10

Crystal, shattered into a million tiny shards, blanketed the tiled floor. Penny shrieked, a long, shrill scream that emanated from some place deep within her.

"The glass! The glass!" As much as she tried, she couldn't stop herself from screaming.

"Penelope!" Grandmother stood at the entrance of the conservatory.

"No, the glass!"

"Take control of yourself!" Grandmother was distraught.

"Now Penny, there's no harm done." Mrs. Meighen and the guests gathered around the conservatory entrance. Their eyes bore a hole through Penny. "But look, your dress has a stain on it. Margie, Margie." Mrs. Meighen's voice was calm and gracious. She waved her hand at one of the maids. "Take Miss Penny into the kitchen and see to her dress."

No, no, they didn't understand. Penny stood, riveted to the spot. The glass! It lay around her feet—bits of glass, each one gleaming like a steel dagger, each one capable of blinding, killing.

"Penelope, whatever is wrong with you?" Grandmother seemed confused.

"Now, now, come on, my dear." Mrs. Meighen put her arm around Penny. "Just follow Margie and she'll have you fixed up in a moment."

Penny took a step. Glass crunched like gravel under her feet. They didn't understand! People in Halifax . . . the explosion . . . everyone in front of their windows. The glass! It went into their bodies, their eyes! She took another step, and another, until at last she was beyond the smashed glass. Shivers went up and down her body, then shame crept up her spine until she was bent over.

"Penelope!" Grandmother called out. But Penny was too ashamed to answer. Instead, with her head down, she followed the maid past Grandmother, past all the men, past all the ladies, down the hall, then down the stairs into the kitchen.

"Just you wait here, Miss. I'll get a cloth." Margie, the maid, left her standing in a gigantic kitchen. Cooks and under-cooks and kitchen maids scurried about, upstairs maids and servants darted every which way. Everyone seemed to be yelling. Penny swallowed hard.

"Margie, take this tray upstairs," a man in a black suit hollered.

"I have to see to her." Margie pointed a finger at Penny.

"I'll look after her. Off you go. Smartly, girl." The man bristled.

"You there." He pointed to a kitchen maid.

"See to her." This time he pointed to Penny.

Her face flaming, Penny stared down at her dress, to her shoes, to the floor. The man heaved a great silver tray onto his shoulder and barged through swinging doors. The girl he yelled at didn't give Penny so much as a glance. She just turned back to the stove and stirred several enormous pots with an equally enormous wooden spoon.

Penny crept into a corner of the massive kitchen and waited. The red stain on her pale-yellow dress seemed to have settled into one large, drippy blotch. The maid did not reappear. Nor did the man in the black suit. Tentatively, one small step at a time, Penny crept over to one of the sinks and dabbed her dress with a damp cloth. The stain didn't dissolve. It got worse! It seemed to leak and spread. It wasn't red any more, it was pink, and larger. It looked like washed-out blood!

If only she could get away. Maybe she could run outside and wait in the car with Arthur. But where was outside? Penny's eyes darted around the kitchen. She was in the basement, that was clear enough. There were stairs to her left. Not the same stairs she had come down, but then, she didn't want to go back to the main rooms. No one had noticed her coming into the kitchen, so they'd hardly miss her leaving. Slowly, Penny backed away and began climbing the narrow, curving steps. She trailed her hand along the wall. It was dark and, with each step, darker still. Should she go back?

Then suddenly the stairs stopped, just like that! Stairs had to lead somewhere, or what was the point? Penny pushed the wall in front of her. If only she could see properly. She pushed again. This time it budged! It was a door of sorts. She brushed back the hair that had fallen into her eyes. Where was her new ribbon? No matter. With her shoulder square against the moving wall, Penny gave it a mighty shove. The wall gave way and the passage was instantly filled with light. She had done it!

"Hello, who is this? Gentlemen, your attention please. A little guest has emerged from the wall."

The room was filled with men and their cigars.

CHAPTER Nº 11

Penny raced up the steps to her grandmother's house and, gripping the polished brass handle, shoved open the door. She caught sight of Sally's gaping mouth as she bolted past her towards the stairs.

"Miss!" Sally scrambled up the steps behind Penny. "Miss!"

"I have to see my aunt." Penny, breathless, stopped on the upstairs landing. She wiped her face with her sleeve and spread the tears all over until her whole face was damp.

"The doctor's been, miss. He gave your aunt a sleeping draft. She'll not be awake again this night."

"Oh no." Desolate, Penny hung her head. What should she do? Grandmother hadn't talked to her all the way home. Not a word. Not even to scold her. One of the men, grinning and smelling of tobacco, had taken her by the hand and led her down the great staircase to the guests below in the grand salon. They had tittered, and some had even laughed. How could they not? There she was, her hair a red haystack, walking down the great staircase with an enormous pink stain running down her dress. And there was Grandmother, standing at the bottom of the staircase, her face as white as chalk, her eyes wide with alarm, and her lips pulled so tight they had all but disappeared.

Sally cocked her ear towards the stairs. They could both hear the front door close.

"Your grandmother will want to see you, I'll wager." She cast a sorry glance at Penny's soiled dress. "I'll just go tend to her."

There she was, her hair a red haystack, walking down the great staircase with an enormous pink stain running down her dress.

"Sally?" Penny looked up. But Sally was gone again, like Alice through the looking glass. She had to talk to her. She couldn't bear to see Grandmother again tonight, to hear her criticisms. "Sally?"

Penny noticed a door swaying. She ran towards it and gave it a sharp shove. Oh, a staircase! So that was how Sally kept appearing and reappearing. And that explained those stairs at Mrs. Meighen's house, too! They weren't back stairs, they were servants' stairs!

"Sally?" Penny peered down the staircase. Sally must have gone down, but she heard voices overhead.

"Sally, are you there?" Slowly she began to climb to the next floor, where she paused.

"Can't think what Madam had in mind having that child come to live here."

Penny raced up a few more tiny steps, pressed her back flat against the wall, and held her breath. Who was that talking? The cook, maybe?

"I don't care if she has Underhill blood. It will

take more than that to make a lady out of that one."

The door beneath her opened and Penny, hardly breathing, watched the backs of two women dressed in caps and aprons as they tromped down the stairs. It didn't matter who was speaking and it didn't matter who was listening, everyone was talking about her. Everyone knew that she was a silly, stupid girl and that she didn't belong anywhere. It was all so unfair. Why? Why her? She flew up the rest of the tiny steps and burst through a small door at the top.

And then, for the second time that day, Penny screamed.

CHAPTER Nº 12

Penny took sharp, shallow breaths. Her eyes darted about, trying to take everything in at once. Bits of evening light filtered through small, round windows under the eaves. They were stained glass—red, blue, yellow—and made faded pools of colour on the wood floor. In the gloom she could just make out the shape of a horse's head, a dust cloth, curly yellow hair, and the very tip of a gleaming sword.

She turned towards the stairs and listened as the clomp, clomp of feet echoed along the passage below her. Go back. Go back. But to what?

Penny caught her breath and strained to see what surrounded her. The sloped roof above was ribbed and the great beams curved inward, like the belly of a ship. A small oil lamp and a pack of wooden matches stood on a tiny, three-legged table. Penny twisted the wick, lit the lamp, then held it up.

Be brave. Be brave. But she wasn't brave, and her legs shook so hard the lamp in her hand flickered. It cast a pool of pale light over something long and thin. With all the courage she could muster, Penny reached over and snatched the length of cloth that was draped over it.

It was a rocking horse! It was blue with a leather saddle studded with jewels. Slowly, Penny inched forward, one hand holding the lamp, the other out in front of her to ward off—well, just in case. One by one, she yanked at dust covers that covered all sorts of mysterious objects. One by one, they fell to the ground.

And then she knew! How obvious! They were

toys, all toys! Trucks, books, even a rocking chair. There was a dollhouse filled with furniture. And over there, a castle with armed guards ready to protect their princess, who stood, sword in hand, on top of a tower. There were drums, too, and blocks, and a whole shelf of dolls. A book of poems was propped up beside the dollhouse. Her hands trembled. Penny opened the book to the first page. Elizabeth Underhill was printed neatly on the upper corner. Mama.

"Oh, Mama." Penny picked up a doll, pressed it tight against her, and crumpled to the floor. Tears fell down her face like pearls tumbling off a string. "Mama, please help me."

"She's here! She's here!"

Penny awoke with a start. What? What was wrong? Where was she?

"I found her! Oh, Miss." Sally fell to her knees in front of Penny. Her cap was askew and her nut-brown hair lay in a tangled mess around her shoulders. "We've been looking for you for ever so long. Your grandmother is frantic."

Penny struggled to sit up. "I didn't mean to . . . I just . . ."

Someone was running up the steps towards them. Each step made a thump that seemed to vibrate through the whole attic.

"Where is she? Where is my granddaughter!" Grandmother, her face contorted with fear, clutched the frame of the door and panted. One hand clutched the front of her long, black dress as she stumbled forward. "Are you all right?" She could hardly catch her breath.

"Yes, Grandmother." Penny, curled up as tight as a cooked shrimp, huddled under a thin blanket.

"Are you sure? Are you very sure? Sally, bring me another lamp. Hurry." Grandmother's hands ran over Penny's face.

"I'm sure." Penny bent her head over her

"Where is my granddaughter!" Grandmother, her face contorted with fear, clutched the frame of the door and panted.

knees. What had she done now?

"Ohhh." Grandmother let out a low, sad moan, then thumped down on a steamer trunk. "Thank goodness." Her hands covered an ashen face.

Arthur, panting and puffing, stood at the attic's entrance.

"Have ya' found her then?"

"Yes, Arthur, tell everyone that Miss Penelope is fine." Grandmother, still too weary to sit straight, tried to collect herself.

"Yes, ma'am."

"Here ya go, ma'am." Sally returned with a large, bright lamp. She held it out straight, so that she looked more like a travelling lighthouse than a maid.

"Thank you, Sally. Leave us, please."

Sally dithered, apparently unsure whether her elderly employer really wanted to be left to sit in a dusty old attic!

"That will be all." Grandmother, exhausted beyond measure, waved her away.

"Grandmother," Penny clutched the blanket

and mumbled, "I didn't mean . . ."

"I thought that you had run away." Grandmother's voice was wispy and faint.

"But I didn't run away, I just meant to hide for a little while. I'm sorry, Grandmother. I didn't mean to upset you. I just found this place by accident! And then I found Mama's things. They are Mama's, aren't they?"

Startled, Grandmother looked around the attic.

"Did they belong to Mama?" Penny's voice was barely above a whisper.

"Yes." Grandmother reached over and picked up the yellow-haired doll. "I remember this one. What was her name? It started with M." Grandmother's voice quavered, and her hands shook so badly that the doll's eyes fluttered open and closed. "I remember now—Martha. Her name is Martha." She searched her sleeve for a hanky and, in an uncustomary and unladylike manner, blew her nose. "I can still see your mother, clear as day, running across the lawn, with Martha in tow." The memory brought a small, wistful smile to the old woman's face.

"Emily had a doll almost like her, but she was lost in the explosion."

"Your sister ... would you like to send your sisters some of your mother's toys?"

"Could we?" Penny felt something unfamiliar spread across her face—a smile.

"Yes, and new ones, too, if you'd like."

"Really? Could we really?"

Grandmother nodded, then looked around at the familiar toys, one by one. The rocking horse, the dollhouse, the castle.

"That trunk has many of your mother's clothes in it. I expect we could put Mrs. Hoffman to the test and see if she could bring one or two up-to-date."

"For me?"

"Yes, of course." Grandmother stowed her hanky in her sleeve and made an effort to sit straight. Still, her face, soft with tears, gave her away.

"Thank you." Penny clasped Martha to her and tried not to cry.

"Penelope—Penny, I have . . . I have made mistakes in my life . . . with your mother. When she ran away . . . to marry your father . . . I became angry. I suppose I was a bit angry with you, too, when you first arrived. You are so like her, you see." Grandmother clutched her hands tight, as if waiting for a pain to pass. "I wanted her to marry well. I wanted her to be happy."

"But, Grandmother, I know Mama was happy." The memory of Mama and Papa dancing in their kitchen floated up in Penny's mind like a bubble. "She loved us all. Well, she didn't get to know Maggie, but she would have loved her. I know she would have. I could tell you about my sisters . . . that is, if you want . . ."

"I'd like to hear all about them."

"And Papa, too?"

"Yes, tell me about your father, too." Grandmother spoke softly. "Perhaps one day he may find a way to forgive an old lady. I've often wondered if your mother ever did."

"Mama loved you. I know she did."

"How do you know that?" Grandmother, astonished, half-afraid, turned and looked at Penny.

"Because she gave me your name! That's how I know."

Unchecked tears fell down Grandmother's face.

"Grandma?" Penny reached for her grandmother's arm. "Oh, Grandma, please don't cry. It will be all right. You'll see."

She turned, reached out for Penny, and took her in her arms.

"My girl, my dear girl."

ENDNOTES

Penny lives in an area of Montreal once called the Golden Square Mile. The boundaries are Atwater Street, Parc Avenue, Mount Royal, and de la Gauchetière. There have been changes since it first emerged in 1850, and many of the mansions have been torn down and replaced with modern office buildings. But some of the great houses still exist, thanks to a few Montrealers who love their city dearly and protect it ardently.

Penny and her grandmother live at 1110 Pine Avenue West, at the corner of Peel Street. It's called the Lady Meredith House. In 1941, Lady Meredith donated the house to the Royal Victoria Hospital. It was acquired by McGill University in 1960. A terrible fire gutted the interior in 1990, but much of the downstairs has been restored.

The Meighen House, on 1440 Drummond Street, is now called the Mount Stephen Club. It is a private club, but public seating in their exclusive dining rooms and thrilling tours are still possible. (Yes, you really can see the stairs Penny walked down!)

Ravenscrag, or the Hugh Allan House, 1025 Pine Avenue, is now part of the Royal Victoria Hospital and called the Allan Memorial Institute. And it's true, the Allan family really did lose two daughters on the Lusitania and a son in the trenches of World War I.

Acknowledgements:

Mount Stephen Club, Montreal. Jean-Pierre Amberg,
General Manager. Jacques Brunet, House Master.

Johanne King, historical expert.

Canadian Pacific Railway Archives, Jo-Anne Colby.

McGill University, Meredith House. Scot De Jong,
Executive Director, Faculty of Medicine.

Burlington Public Library, Andrea Gordon, Manager,
Children's and Youth Services. And, tout la gang!

Barbara Berson, Senior Editor, Penguin.

Ian (D. J.) McKay, Father and unpaid editor.

Catherine Marjoribanks, Editor.

Katie Parsons, junior reader.

And most especially, Janet Kitz, Halifax, Nova Scotia.

Dear Reader,

Welcome back to the continuing adventures of Our Canadian Girl! It's been a very exciting year for us here at Penguin, publishing new stories of eight different girls, with more on the way! The best part of this past year, though, has been the wonderful letters we've received from readers like you, telling us your favourite Our Canadian Girl story, which parts you liked the most. Best of all, you told us which stories you would like to read, and we were amazed! There are so many remarkable stories in Canadian history. It seems that wherever we live, great stories live too, in our towns and cities, on our rivers and mountains. Thank you so much for sharing them.

So please, stay in touch. Write letters, log on to our website, let us know what you think of Our Canadian Girl. We're listening.

Sincerely,
    Barbara Berson

Canada's

1608
Samuel de Champlain establishes the first fortified trading post at Quebec.

1759
The British defeat the French in the Battle of the Plains of Abraham.

1812
The United States declares war against Canada.

1845
The expedition of Sir John Franklin to the Arctic ends when the ship is frozen in the pack ice; the fate of its crew remains a mystery.

1869
Louis Riel leads his Métis followers in the Red River Rebellion.

1871
British Columbia joins Canada.

1755
The British expel the entire French population of Acadia (today's Maritime provinces), sending them into exile.

1776
The 13 Colonies revolt against Britain, and the Loyalists flee to Canada.

1837
Calling for responsible government, the Patriotes, following Louis-Joseph Papineau, rebel in Lower Canada; William Lyon Mackenzie leads the uprising in Upper Canada.

1867
New Brunswick, Nova Scotia and the United Province of Canada come together in Confederation to form the Dominion of Canada.

1870
Manitoba joins Canada. The Northwest Territories become an official territory of Canada.

1784
Rachel

Timeline

1885
At Craigellachie, British Columbia, the last spike is driven to complete the building of the Canadian Pacific Railway.

1898
The Yukon Territory becomes an official territory of Canada.

1914
Britain declares war on Germany, and Canada, because of its ties to Britain, is at war too.

1918
As a result of the Wartime Elections Act, the women of Canada are given the right to vote in federal elections.

1945
World War II ends conclusively with the dropping of atomic bombs on Hiroshima and Nagasaki.

1873
Prince Edward Island joins Canada.

1896
Gold is discovered on Bonanza Creek, a tributary of the Klondike River.

1905
Alberta and Saskatchewan join Canada.

1917
In the Halifax harbour, two ships collide, causing an explosion that leaves more than 1,600 dead and 9,000 injured.

1939
Canada declares war on Germany seven days after war is declared by Britain and France.

1949
Newfoundland, under the leadership of Joey Smallwood, joins Canada.

1896
Emily

1885
Marie-Claire

1918
Penelope

Check out the
Our Canadian Girl website

Fun Stuff

- E-cards
- Prizes
- Activities
- Poll

Fan Area

- Guest Book
- Photo Gallery
- Downloadable *Our Canadian Girl* Tea Party Kit

Features on the girls and more!

www.ourcanadiangirl.ca